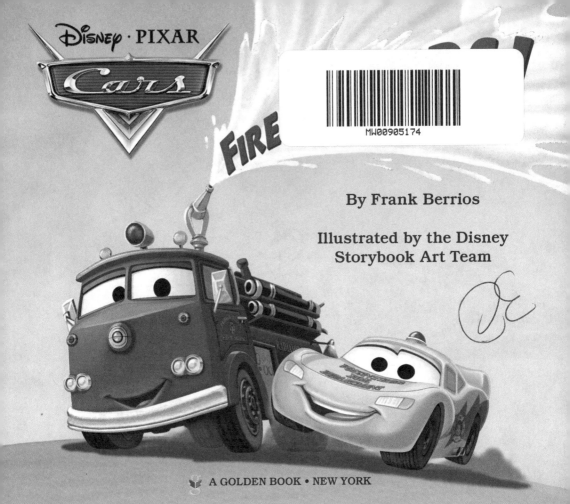

Disney · PIXAR

Cars

FIRE

By Frank Berrios

Illustrated by the Disney
Storybook Art Team

A GOLDEN BOOK • NEW YORK

Materials and characters from the movie *Cars*. Copyright © 2014 Disney•Pixar. Disney•Pixar elements © Disney•Pixar, not including underlying vehicles owned by third parties; and, if applicable: Chevrolet Impala is a trademark of General Motors; Hudson Hornet is a trademark of Chrysler LLC; Jeep® and the Jeep® grille design are registered trademarks of Chrysler LLC; Ferrari Elements produced under license of Ferrari S.p.A. FERRARI, the PRANCING HORSE device, all associated logos and distinctive designs are property of Ferrari S.p.A. The body designs of the Ferrari cars are protected as Ferrari property under design, trademark and trade dress regulations; FIAT is a trademark of FIAT S.p.A.; Mercury and Model T are registered trademarks of Ford Motor Company; Porsche is a trademark of Porsche; Sarge's rank insignia design used with the approval of the U.S. Army; and Volkswagen trademarks, design patents and copyrights are used with the approval of the owner, Volkswagen AG. Background inspired by the Cadillac Ranch by Ant Farm (Lord, Michels and Marquez) © 1974. All rights reserved. Published in the United States by Golden Books, an imprint of Random House Children's Books, a division of Random House LLC, 1745 Broadway, New York, NY 10019, and in Canada by Random House of Canada Limited, Toronto, Penguin Random House Companies, in conjunction with Disney Enterprises, Inc. Golden Books, A Golden Book, A Little Golden Book, the G colophon, and the distinctive gold spine are registered trademarks of Random House LLC.
randomhouse.com/kids
ISBN 978-0-7364-3169-9 (trade) – ISBN 978-0-7364-3229-0 (ebook)
Printed in the United States of America
10 9 8 7 6 5 4 3 2 1

Radiator Springs was once a sleepy town. Now racing fans from all over the globe were eager to see Lightning McQueen's home. But more cars meant that some changes had to be made.

"Red, with all these folks to look after, you're going to need some help," Sheriff said to the town's only fire truck.

Everyone agreed, and Sarge offered to help Red
put together a group of firefighting volunteers.

"When a fire breaks out, someone has to ring the alarm," said Sarge. "In an emergency, you've got to move fast!"

"I can do that!" shouted Lightning. But the red racer was too fast! He bumped into the alarm and sent the bell flying through the air.

"Looks like we're going to need a new bell," whispered Doc.

"Next drill!" barked Sarge. "Luigi! Guido! Let me see you raise that ladder up to the roof."

"Pronto!" Luigi replied. But Guido lost his grip on the ladder and it toppled over.

"Incoming!" yelled Sarge, narrowly avoiding the falling ladder.

Next, the volunteers had to practice using
a fire hydrant.

"Mater, hook up the hose and aim it," ordered
Sarge. "Ramone, open the hydrant."

The new recruits sprang into action, but
Mater got tangled in the hose.

"Look out!" yelled Mater as a flood of water soaked Sarge.

"Next time, turn on the water *after* you hook up the hose," sputtered Sarge.

Soon Radiator Springs had its very own
fire brigade, but it needed lots of work.

"Don't worry," said Lightning. "Firefighting is a lot like being part of a pit crew. It takes teamwork—everybody has to do their part."

Then Red got some exciting news. The fire brigade
had been chosen to lead the annual Radiator Springs
Day parade!

"This calls for a wash-and-wax," suggested
Lightning.

"We're gonna need more than that," Ramone replied. "It's time for me to start working my magic! That is, if it's okay with you, Chief."

Red couldn't wait! He raced over to Ramone's body shop so he could be first in line for a new paint job.

Before long, each member of the crew had a shiny new coat of paint and a Radiator Springs Fire Brigade logo.

"Look at us!" exclaimed Luigi.

At Luigi's tire shop, Luigi and Guido gave the entire team new wheels!

"Now we are ready for the parade!" Luigi said proudly.

The next day, Lightning woke up early and went looking for Mater, but the tow truck was nowhere to be found. As Lightning made his way over to the firehouse, he smelled smoke. Something was on fire! He raced to sound the alarm, but Red beat him to it.

Within seconds, Red was racing toward the smoke, his siren blaring and lights flashing. Members of the fire brigade arrived just behind him.

"This is not a drill!" Lightning shouted to the team. "Man your stations!"

"Stay back, folks," warned Fillmore. His job was to keep the crowd away from the fire.

Guido unloaded a fire hose, and Luigi connected it to a hydrant. Ramone got ready to release the water. Everyone did their job—but where was Mater?

Luigi and Guido took control of the hose. On Red's signal, Ramone turned on the water. Luigi and Guido sprayed water on the smoke cloud from one side, while Red hosed it down from the other.

"It's Mater!" Lightning exclaimed when the smoke cleared. "Are you all right?"

"Oh, yeah," replied Mater. "Just a little wet is all. I was so nervous about the parade, I got overheated."

"Hey, we did it!" said Lightning. "We put out a fire!"
"Great teamwork," said Sheriff just as Lizzie
came put-putting along.

"Am I late for the parade?" asked Lizzie. "Oh, well. Happy Radiator Springs Day, everybody!" she shouted, showering them all with confetti.

"Hooray!" cheered the crowd as the parade began, led by the Radiator Springs Fire Brigade. With bravery and teamwork, the town's volunteers had turned into honest-to-goodness firefighters! Red could not have been more proud of his new firefighting team.